NUFF SAID

NUFF SAID

another tale of Bluebell Wood

Herbie Brennan

illustrated by Ross Collins

BLOOMSBURY
CHILDREN'S
BOOKS

Published by Bloomsbury, New York and London
Distributed to the trade by St. Martin's Press

Library of Congress Cataloging-in-Publication Data:
Brennan, Herbie.
Nuff said: another tale of Bluebell Wood / Herbie Brennan;
illustrated by Ross Collins. – 1st U.S. ed. p.cm. Sequel to: Fairy Nuff.
Summary: Between hungry African ants, worried Javanese termites, hot weather,
and an error by a dyslexic builder, Fairy Nuff has his hands full on the day of
his extravagant garden party even before the evil Widow Buhiss arrives.
[1. Parties—Fiction. 2. Castles—Fiction. 3. Ants—Fiction. 4. Termites—Fiction. 5.
England—Fiction. 6. Humorous stories.] I. Collins, Ross, ill. II. Title.
PZ7.B75153 Nu 2002
[Fic]—dc21
2001043905

ISBN: 1-58234-771-9

Printed in Great Britain
First U.S. Edition

1 3 5 7 9 10 8 6 4 2

Bloomsbury USA Children's Books
175 Fifth Avenue
New York, New York 10010

For darling Jacks – H.B.

One

It all started in Java when a termite named Albert met a termite in a turban.

"What gift do you seek, my son?" asked the termite in the turban, seated cross-legged for his meditation.

Albert blinked. "I'm not here for a gift," he said. "I'm here to chew wood. Chew-chew, chew-chew."

"He who does not seek shall find," the termite in the turban told him sagely. He sniffed. "I think I'll give you prophecy."

So saying, he waved one of his legs that wasn't crossed.

It was as if a window opened up in Albert's mind. He saw the world's first

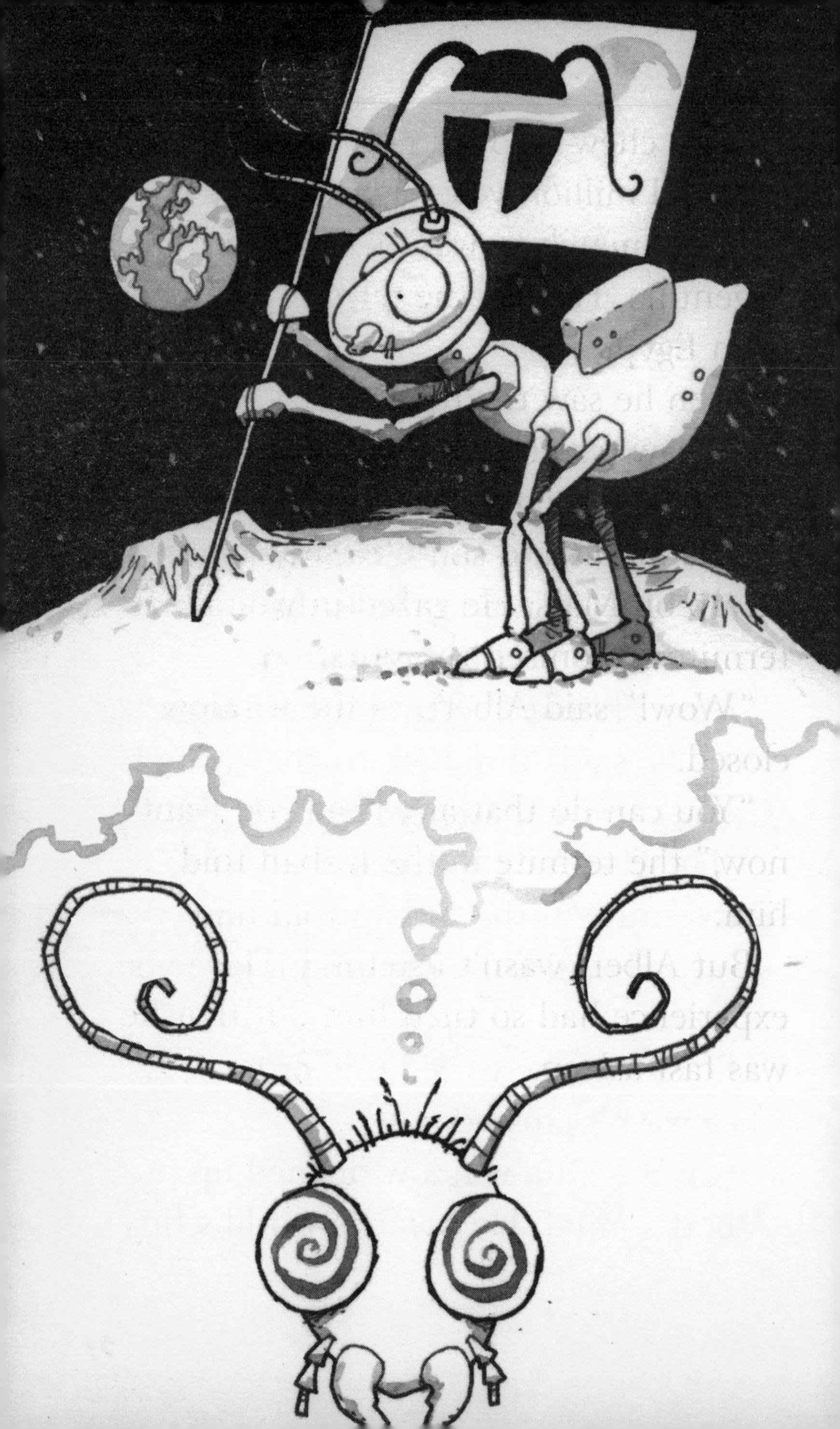

termite chew through a dinosaur two hundred million years ago. He saw termites march to war on the plains of Argentina. He saw the termite exodus from Egypt.

Then he saw the future.

He saw termite civilisations rise and fall. He watched the first termite land on the moon and saw a termite colony set up on Mars. He gazed in wonder as termites colonised the stars.

"Wow!" said Albert, as the window closed.

"You can do that any time you want now," the termite in the turban told him.

But Albert wasn't listening. The experience had so tired him out that he was fast asleep.

Two

Albert woke surrounded by a group of fellow workers.

One of them (named Ilbert) poked him with a feeler. "Come on, Albert, get a move on."

"Work to be done," another said. "Wood to be chewed. Chew-chew, chew-chew!"

A third termite by the name of Gilbert pushed forward. "Looks poorly to me," he said. "Let's eat him."

They huddled for a confab. One of the larger workers, a soft-hearted termite named Ulbert, sniffed. "Don't usually eat them until they're dead," he said.

Gilbert shrugged several of his shoulders. "Poorly ... dead ... what's the difference? I say we eat him while he's fresh."

"I'm not poorly," Albert said.

"You sure?" Gilbert frowned. "You don't think we should eat you anyway?"

"No," said Albert firmly. "I was just taking a little nap. Let's all eat something else. Chew-chew, chew-chew." He made a sharp right turn and bit into the wall. Within minutes, they were eating out a brand-new corridor.

Later as they chewed a decorative niche, Albert could contain himself no longer. "Know what?" he said. "I can see the future!"

"Yes," said Gilbert, "and I look just like Dolly Parton."

"No, seriously," said Albert, who didn't know who Dolly Parton was.

Ilbert spat some wood politely on the floor. "Time is a river," he said philosophically. "The past is gone, the future yet to come. There is only the Eternal Now. Thus the future must be hidden from all but the Great Termite in the Sky."

"No, seriously," Albert said again.

"Prove it," Gilbert snapped.

"How can I prove it?" Albert asked.

Gilbert fixed Albert with a gimlet eye. "Just tell us something that will happen tomorrow," he said.

Albert blinked then closed his eyes. After a while he said, "Our home will be chopped down and cut up tomorrow."

They looked at him blankly.

Eyes still closed, Albert said, "We will all make a long sea journey to somewhere with a Labour government." He opened his eyes and grinned triumphantly.

Gilbert pursed his mandibles. "That'll never happen!" he exclaimed.

Miffed, Albert said, "If I'm wrong, you can eat me – how about that?"

His fellow termites looked him up and down.

"Yes," said Gilbert slowly. "Yes, we will."

Three

Next day the sun came up like thunder in the Horrible Outside. Albert washed his face and chewed his way out of the tiny cell where he had spent the night. Then he walked down to the communal breakfast room.

"Good morning!" he called cheerfully. "Nice day for a chew. Chew-chew, chew-chew!"

There was silence in the breakfast room. Seventy-eight million termite eyes turned to stare at him.

"What?" asked Albert. "What? What? Why are you all looking at me like that?"

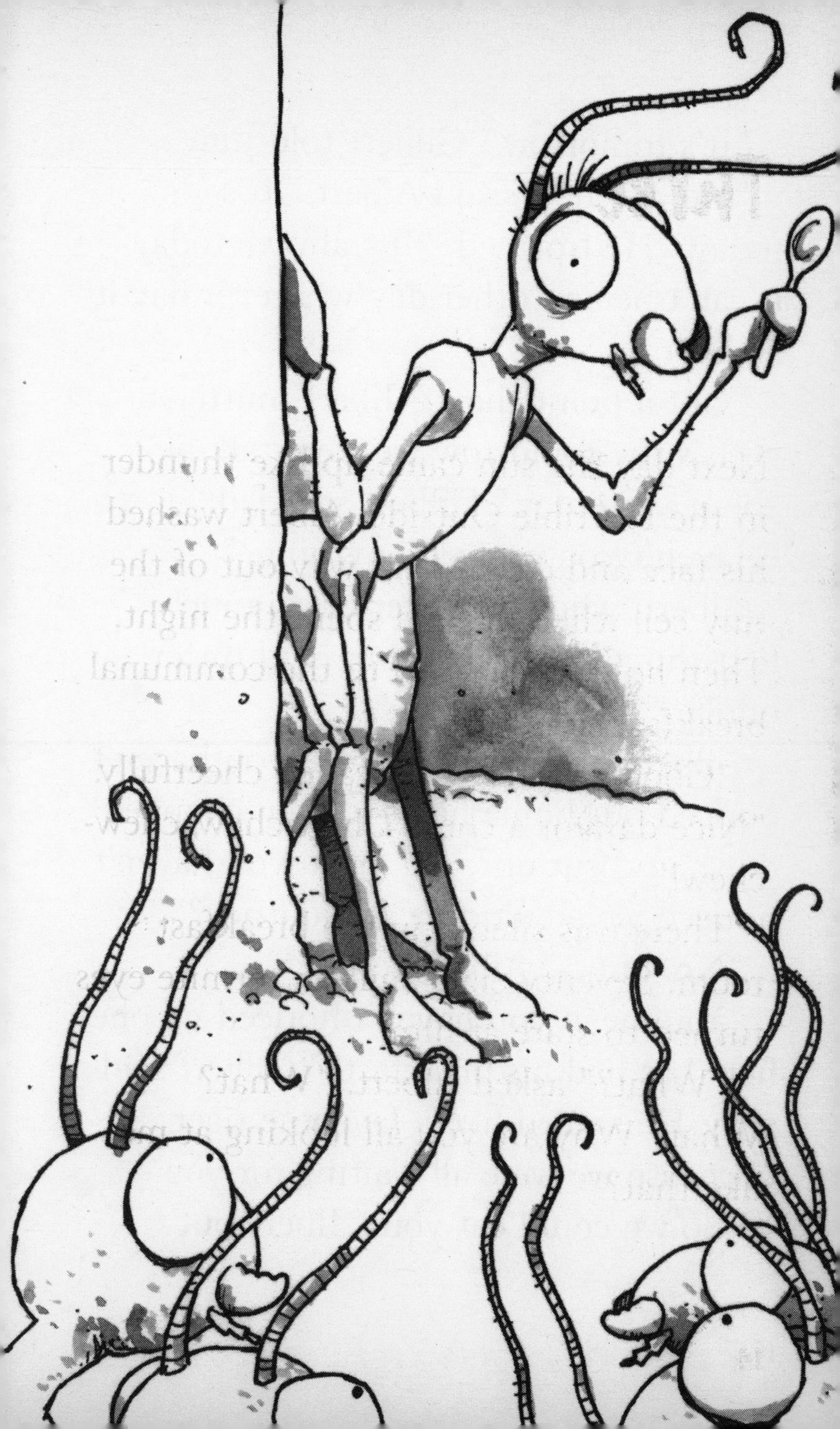

"It's tomorrow," Gilbert told him.

"No, it's not," said Albert. "It's today." He frowned. "It's always today – it can't be any other day whatever day it is. Ever."

"Got a point there," Ilbert muttered.

"It's the tomorrow we were talking about yesterday," Gilbert scowled. "Haven't you noticed anything?"

Albert, who was never up to much first thing in the morning, said uncertainly, "No ..."

Gilbert sniffed. "You mean you haven't noticed our home has not been chopped down and cut up? You mean you haven't noticed we aren't on a sea journey?"

"No, but—" Albert began.

"You mean you haven't noticed no one here has had his breakfast?" Gilbert said slyly. He smiled like a Javanese tiger. "Because we were all waiting for you."

"So we could eat you," Ilbert put

in helpfully.

"Just a minute," Albert said firmly. "This may be yesterday's tomorrow, but it's still today's today. And very early at that."

"What's that got to do with anything?" asked Gilbert sourly. He hated late breakfasts.

"It's got everything to do with everything," Albert told him. "There's lots of time for us to be chopped down, cut up and transported by sea. I didn't say it would happen early, did I? I didn't say it would happen before breakfast. I didn't say it would happen first thing in the morning."

Ulbert, the soft-hearted termite, said, "No he didn't. You have to give him that."

"Didn't say it wouldn't either," put in Ilbert.

"Look," said Gilbert, who was suffering from low blood sugar and needed to eat somebody, "why don't we let the King decide?"

"Let the King decide!" chanted thirty-nine million termite voices.

Four

When thirty-nine million termites
chanted all together, the tree they lived
in shook. The shaking caused its leaves
to rustle. This caught the eye of two
Javanese lumberjacks working in the
Horrible Outside.

"What about that one?" the nearest
asked (in Javanese). "It's shaking so badly
it's likely to fall down soon anyway."

"Looks good to me," the other nodded.

They advanced on the tree with axes
and chainsaws.

"To the King! To the King!" chanted
thirty-nine million termite voices on the
Beautiful Inside.

Despite his protests, Albert found himself swept up by a tide of termites who carried him through a maze of galleries to the Royal Chamber of King Ethelbert.

The King looked up in alarm as his subjects swarmed in. "This isn't a revolution, is it? Because if it is, I won't have it."

"No, no, Sire," Gilbert smarmed at him. "We just need a ruling on a point of law."

"Queen does points of law," said Ethelbert shortly. "I just sit here and look pretty."

"Yes, Sire, but she's busy laying eggs."

Ethelbert glared. "She's always busy laying eggs." He sniffed. "Oh, well, I suppose I'd better adjudicate. What's the point of law?"

"Albert said we could eat him if our tree wasn't chopped down, cut up and

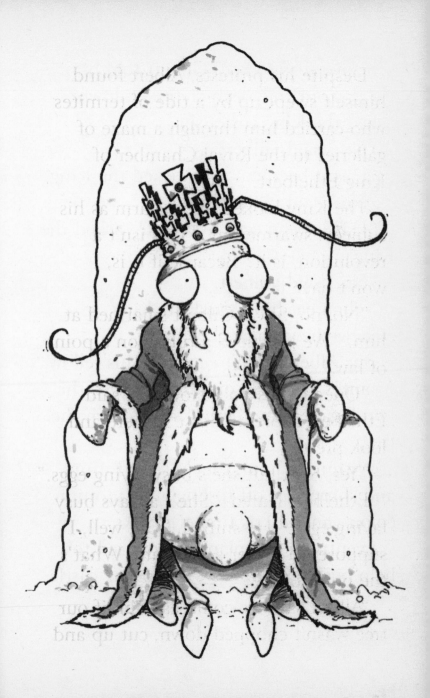

sent overseas today," Gilbert told him.

"Has our tree been chopped down?" asked the King curiously.

"No," said Gilbert.

"Has it been cut up?" asked the King.

"No," said Gilbert.

"Has it been sent overseas?" asked the King.

"No," said Gilbert.

"Then eat him," said the King. "Chew-chew, chew-chew!"

But Albert wasn't eaten. As his fellow termites closed in on him hungrily, the two Javanese lumberjacks cut down the tree.

Within an hour, they'd sawed it up and shipped it off to England (termite colony and all) as timber planks.

Eventually the planks were used to help build Fairy Nuff's exploding castle.

Five

This is how Fairy Nuff came to have an exploding castle.

First he found twenty thousand billion pounds lying about in Bluebell Wood. The twenty thousand billion pounds was not in cash. It was twenty thousand share certificates in an Australian gold mine, each one worth one billion pounds.

Since he didn't trust banks, Fairy Nuff hid nineteen thousand, nine hundred and ninety-nine of the certificates in a hollow tree, which he marked with a large red cross so he wouldn't forget where it was. Then he took the twenty thousandth certificate to his local bank and asked if they could cash it.

The cashier took three days to count out the money and Fairy Nuff trundled it away in a wheelbarrow. When he got back to Bluebell Wood, he set aside one million for pocket money and stuffed the rest into the hollow tree along with the share certificates. He painted another large red cross on the tree just to be sure.

The money actually belonged to someone called Widow Buhiss, but Fairy didn't know that. He should have asked around, of course, but since he wasn't over-blessed with brains he never thought of it.

Widow Buhiss didn't claim her money either. She was locked up in the Tower of London with her groundskeeper Orc and pitbull terrier Gestapo for kidnapping the Queen of England. She spent her time plotting a painful revenge on the person who'd foiled her plot and put her there.

That person, as it happened, was Fairy Nuff. Since he'd earned himself a knighthood for saving the Queen, he decided he would build a nice big castle to go with it.

He planned towers and turrets, secret passages, deep dungeons, stone-flagged corridors, a great hall, a small hall, a banquet hall, a pool hall, a music hall, kitchens, a laundry, a library, showers, saunas, a recording studio, several dozen bathrooms, two hundred bedrooms, stables, stores, a central courtyard, a drawbridge, a portcullis and a moat. Money was no object.

Once the plans were drawn up, Fairy hired a builder called Murphy O'Toole who was thick as a brick, short-sighted and dyslexic.

Murphy O'Toole estimated the castle would take two million, three hundred thousand cut stone blocks – much the same as the Great Pyramid. He reckoned it would also need one hundred and fifty thousand tons of timber and twenty thousand tons of best cement.

Murphy ordered the timber from an endangered rainforest in Java, but found a cheap source of cement at the end of a side road close to Tunbridge Wells. He drove down to collect it late one gloomy autumn afternoon.

There were two factories side by side at the end of the side road close to Tunbridge Wells. One was the Apex Cement Company. The other was the Aqex Fireworks Corporation.

The Apex Cement Company had a large sign outside that said:

The Aqex Firework Corporation had an equally large sign outside that said:

Murphy headed through the gate marked Aqex and loaded up with twenty thousand tons of dark grey powder he thought was premium grade cement. The delivery docket showed the load as 'gunpowder, double strength' but he didn't have his glasses with him.

Murphy drove the gunpowder to Bluebell Wood and dumped it in the clearing where Fairy Nuff's old cottage used to be.

Then his men began to build the castle.

When mixed with sand and water, the gunpowder worked well as cement. Murphy poured eleven thousand tons of it to make a firm foundation. The rest he used as mortar in the walls.

Since money was no object, the building work went quickly and the stone shell of a great castle began to rise above the treetops of Bluebell Wood.

Workmen came and went, smoking cigarettes, lighting fires to boil up cans of tea. Sparks flew off the hobnails in their hobnailed boots. None of this was any problem whatsoever. The cement, while it stayed wet, was safe as houses.

But as autumn turned to winter and winter turned to spring, the weather improved and the gunpowder cement began to dry.

By the time the decorators were ready to move in, Fairy Nuff's castle was a time-bomb waiting to explode.

Six

The decorators finished up towards the end of June. Since June was very hot and dry that year, Fairy Nuff decided he would hold a garden party to celebrate the opening of his brand-new castle.

His PR people drew up a guest list of media personalities, movie stars, peers, politicians, freeloaders and everybody in Fairy Nuff's personal address book. Unfortunately the personal address book happened to include the names of Orc and Widow Buhiss, who'd lived quite close to Fairy Nuff before they were thrown into the Tower of London.

A PR person in a business suit showed the list to Fairy Nuff, but he got bored

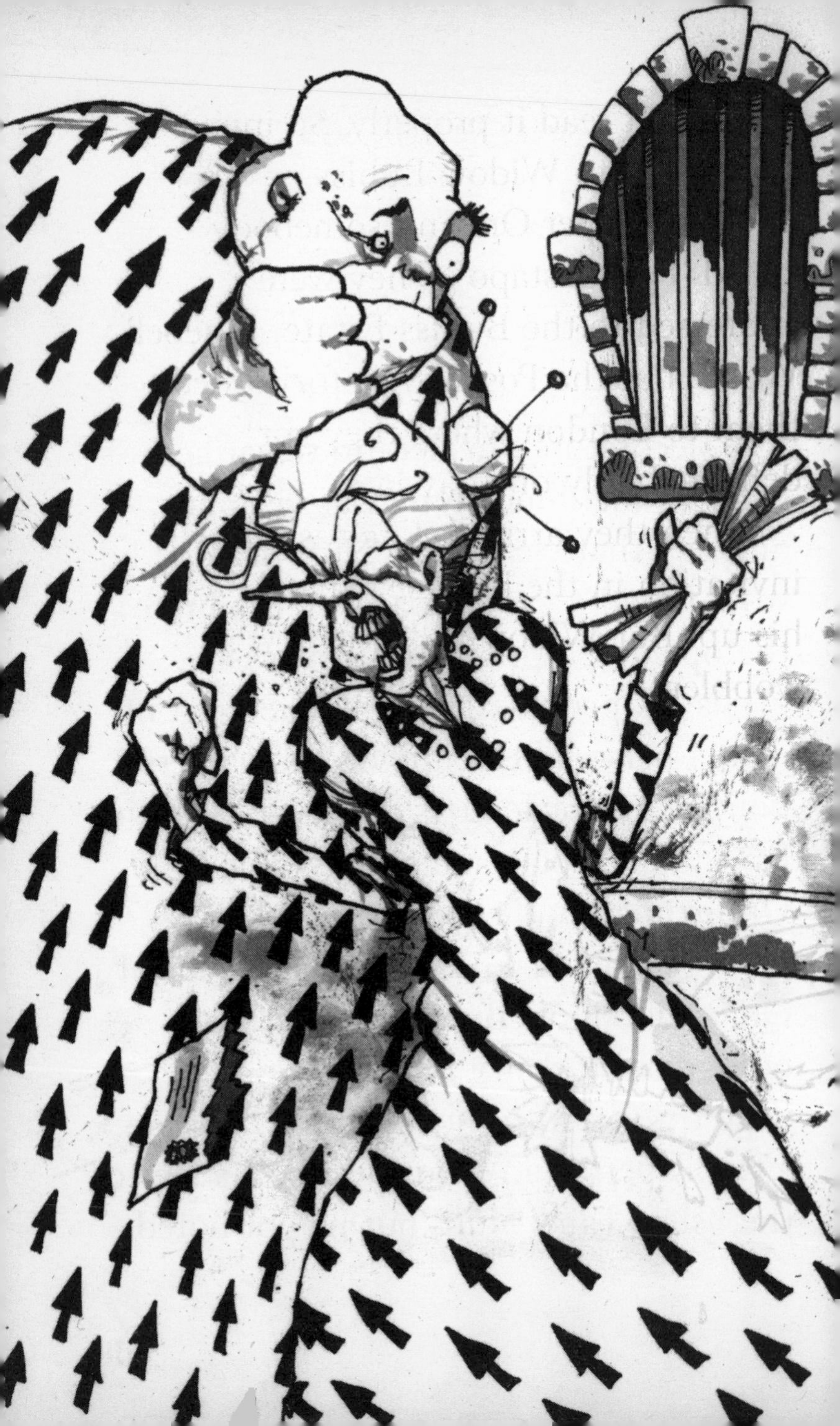

and didn't read it properly. So invitations went to Widow Buhiss, Groundskeeper Orc and somebody called 'P T Gestapo'. They were addressed to the Buhiss Estate, Bluebell Wood, but the Post Office forwarded them to London where they got delivered only one day late.

When they arrived, Orc tossed his invitation in the bin. Gestapo chewed his up. But Widow Buhiss threw a wobbler.

"What's this?" she screamed at no one in particular. "An invitation to a garden party thrown by Fairy Nuff? The boy who foiled my plans and had us locked up in this smelly dungeon?"

"Yus, that boy," Orc confirmed.

"Aaaaaghhhhh!" screamed Widow Buhiss in frustration. She clawed bricks from the walls and danced about. "Aaaaaaghhhhh! Aaaaaaghhhhh! Aaaaaaghhhhhh!"

There was a thunderous knocking on the door of their cell. "What's going on in there?" a guard called out. "Who's making all that noise."

"Aaaaaghhhhh!" shrieked Widow Buhiss, louder than before.

The cell door opened and the guard came in. Widow Buhiss hit him with the last brick she'd clawed from the wall and he fell down like a sack of spuds.

"Freedom!" yelled Widow Buhiss incomprehensibly.

Swiftly she pulled off her prison garb. She stood over the prostrate body for a moment in her vest and knickers – a hideous sight – then kicked him a few times to make sure he was still unconscious. When he didn't move, she started to remove his clothes.

Since he was a Beefeater, he was wearing a red and yellow coat-dress over orange tights and buckled shoes. His trousers, which only came down to the knee, were puffed out like balloons. He had a ruff around his neck, a flat black hat and white gloves.

Everything fitted Widow Buhiss reasonably well, except for the hat which slipped down over her eyes. But she stuffed it with used loo paper and jammed it back on. She kicked the Beefeater again out of badness, then picked up his keys.

"Come on," she snapped at Orc. "We're getting out of here. Keep your eyes down, put this chain around your neck and pretend to be my prisoner."

Orc looked at her gloomily. "Where we going then?" he asked.

"We're going to get Fairy Nuff!" Widow Buhiss told him grimly.

Seven

Since he wanted it to be a very special garden party, Fairy Nuff organised several entertainments to impress his guests.

He booked the BBC West of England Light Orchestra to play for them.

He commissioned a life-size ice sculpture of King Kong climbing the Empire State Building.

He had the castle grounds landscaped by a Zen gardener flown in from Japan.

He hired the entire National State Circus of the People's Republic of China – two hundred and eighty-seven members not counting elephants, pandas and horses.

He bought the old Millennium Dome and had ten thousand men on stand-by to put it up in case of rain.

He persuaded the Red Arrows to do a fly-past upside down.

He ordered a jumbo jet from Richard Branson to fly in transatlantic visitors and paid for Europeans to come in on the Orient Express.

As a way of making overseas guests feel at home, he ordered life-size papier mâché replicas of the Statue of Liberty, the Eiffel Tower, the Parthenon, the Coliseum, the Pyramids, the Swiss Alps and a Belgian chocolate factory. He had Ayers Rock shipped from Australia on temporary loan.

As a focal point, he had the wreck of
the Titanic set up on the croquet lawn.
Beside it he had built a replica of the
Rose Bowl, which he had filled with
water and stocked with goldfish as a
novelty attraction.

For the children, there were round-
the-moon Space Shuttle trips laid on by
NASA and the whole of Disneyland
Paris was brought across from France.

He set up hot dog stands and candy-floss stands and slot machine arcades. He hired troubadours and minstrels, jugglers by the score, fire-eaters, sword-swallowers, thimble-riggers, conjurers, tumblers, quick-change artists, stand-up comedians, raconteurs and party wits.

All this cost a fierce amount of money.

Fairy Nuff told everybody they'd get paid at his garden party.

Eight

A few days before the garden party, the RSVPs started to come in.

The first to arrive was from the American President who said he'd be delighted to attend provided Fairy Nuff covered his expenses.

The British Prime Minister said yes as well, but didn't mention his expenses, probably because he didn't have so far to go.

These replies were followed in quick succession by acceptances from the Irish Taoiseach, the President of France and the Secretary-General of the United Nations.

Seventy-eight of Fairy's favourite pop groups accepted en masse.

FAIRY NUFF
THE CASTLE
BLUEBELL WOOD
ENGLAND

The England football team said they were coming in a coach.

The Queen (who was extremely fond of Fairy Nuff since he'd saved her from Widow Buhiss) sent her regrets but she said she'd have the Poet Laureate read something he'd written specially for the occasion. She enclosed a preview copy for Fairy Nuff's approval.

The poem read:

It's fair enough for Fairy Nuff
To build his castle in a wood
But to invite us to this bean-feast
Seems to make it twice as good
At this terrific garden party
We will no doubt all eat hearty
And be nicely entertained
By people who have lots of brains
The guests have come from miles around
From France, from Germany and Spain
Let fun and games and joy abound
Before they go back home again.
For all this stuff Fairy has paid
We hope he won't go in the red
But if he does there's still enjoyment
Because it gives such high employment
So let us now raise up our glasses
Before another minute passes
And drink a toast to Fairy Nuff
Who really seems to know his stuff.

Fairy Nuff thought it was probably the worst poem he'd ever read, but he gave his approval anyway since he didn't want to offend the Queen. Besides, he quite liked the thought that everybody would have to drink a toast to him when the Poet Laureate finished.

All the media personalities, movie stars, peers, politicians and freeloaders said they'd be delighted to attend.

Widow Buhiss, Orc and P T Gestapo didn't reply at all, so Fairy Nuff never even knew they'd been invited, let alone that they were on their way to get him.

Nine

Before Widow Buhiss left the Tower of London, she visited the Waterloo Barracks, dragging Orc behind her. He made gasping, gagging noises as she jerked the chain around his throat.

No one stopped them as they walked inside, but halfway down the corridor a real Beefeater stepped out.

"Who goes there?" challenged the Beefeater.

"The Keys!" said Widow Buhiss, who'd listened to this nonsense through her dungeon window. She shook the keys she'd stolen from the Beefeater. They made a pleasing jingling sound.

"What's that thing on the end of your

chain?" asked the Beefeater curiously.

"None of your business," Widow Buhiss told him.

The Yeoman Guard was still peering at Orc. "Yes, I know, but I've never seen anything quite like it. Orang-utan? Is it an orang-utan?"

"No, of course not," said Widow Bushiss.

"Mountain gorilla! It's a mountain gorilla!"

"It's not a mountain gorilla either," Widow Buhiss snapped. "Now look—"

But the Beefeater only looked at Orc. "Hey, Harry, come here a minute!" he called over his shoulder.

Another Beefeater appeared. "Good grief, Samuel, what's that?"

"I thought it was a shaved orang-utan or possibly a mountain gorilla," Samuel told him, "but apparently not – at least not according to our colleague here."

"It's never a mountain gorilla," Harry said. "Too ugly and muscular. It might be an alien. You get the most peculiar things in Outer Space. Is it an alien?"

Orc growled slightly, but Widow Buhiss said impatiently, "Yes, it's an alien. Now can we get on with the who goes business? I'm running late."

"Sorry," Samuel said, "I was just a bit startled. I suppose it's for the Royal Menagerie?"

"Yes, that's exactly what it's for. Now, can we do the rest of the who goes business so I can get on the way?"

"We can take that as read," Samuel said and waved her on her way.

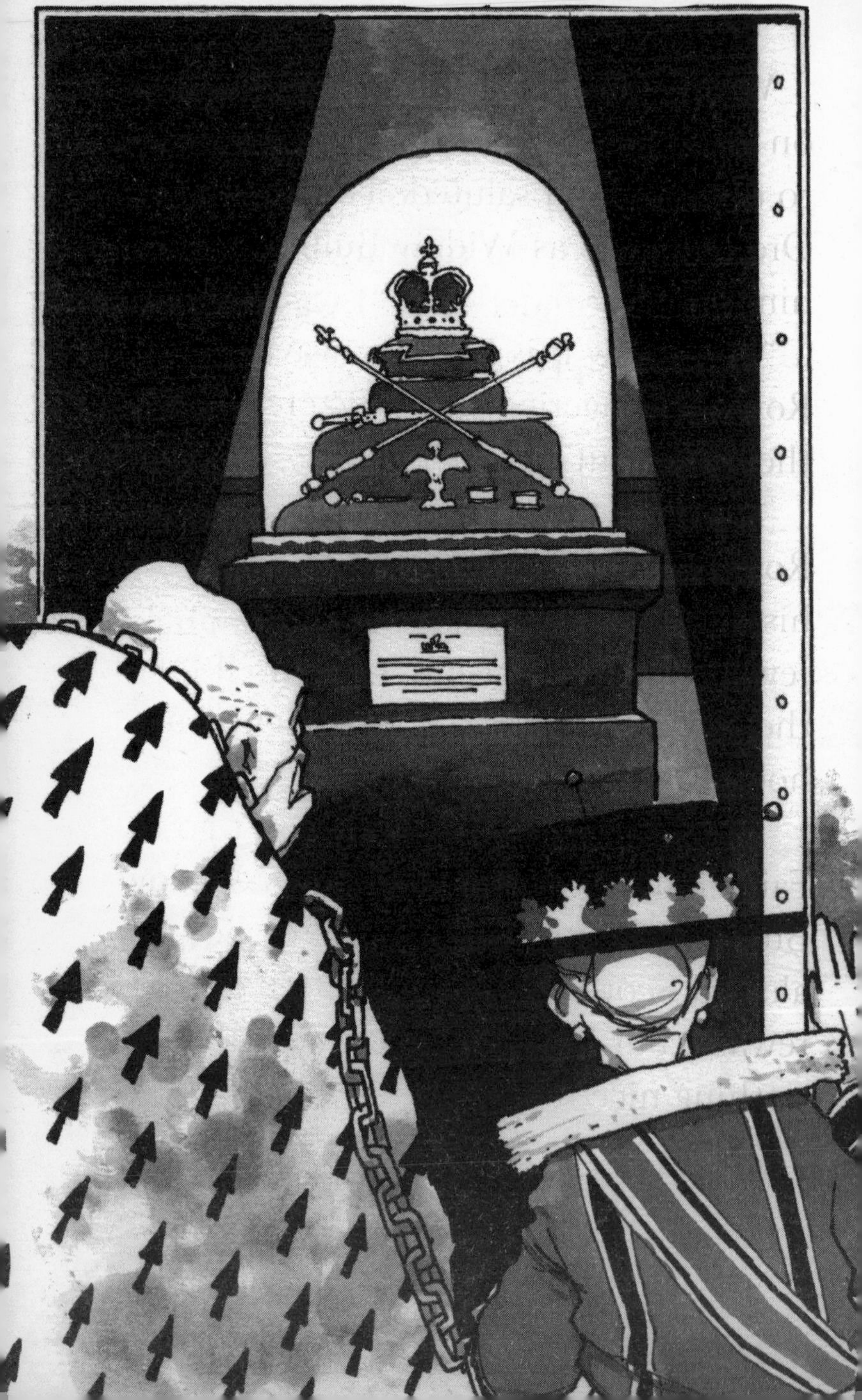

Widow Buhiss marched past jerking on Orc's chain. Harry and Samuel stood to one side and saluted. They stared at Orc curiously as Widow Buhiss dragged him past.

"You know this isn't the way to the Royal Menagerie," Orc muttered once they were out of earshot.

"Of course it's not the way to the Royal Menagerie," Widow Buhiss hissed. "It's the way to the Crown Jewels. I thought we might as well take them while we were in the neighbour-hood."

That's why the Queen couldn't go to Fairy Nuff's garden party. After Widow Buhiss stole her Crown Jewels, she alerted Scotland Yard and offered a reward, but in the meantime she had nothing nice to wear.

Ten

After the tree in Java was cut down, chopped up, turned into timber and shipped to England, the termite colony inside it was divided between a large number of floorboards, several wall timbers and some panelling in Fairy Nuff's exploding castle.

But it didn't stay divided for long.

Termites in each board and timber started to send signals to each other by banging on the walls with tin mugs.

Once contact was made, tunnelling termites began to chew out new corridors. Inside a day and a half, seventeen floorboards were connected up. Inside a week and a half, the whole colony was joined together again.

Despite the disruption, King Ethelbert was quite pleased with himself. His kingdom now extended further than it had in Java and there was lots of wood still left to chew.

He was even more pleased with Albert, who'd predicted the whole thing. So much so he made him the High Imperial Grand Termite Prophet and granted him a pension.

In his new position, Albert no longer had chewing duties and got to wear a chain of office (officially called the Chain of Infinite Protection) that meant nobody could eat him if he took a little nap.

As against that, he couldn't just goof off whenever he felt like it. He had to make one official public prophecy a day and spend the rest of the time doing Tarot readings for the Royal Court.

The official prophecy was a ceremonial occasion. The whole colony gathered to hear it. Those who couldn't squeeze into the Throne Room packed the corridors outside to listen on the public address system.

The first time he made an official prophecy, Albert was very nervous. He dressed in his special black and gold prophet's robes and stepped out, shaking like a leaf, before his audience.

He took seven sacred breaths to steady himself, closed his eyes and waited. Because he was so nervous, absolutely nothing happened.

After a while, the audience got restless.

"I think we should eat him," he heard

Gilbert mutter.

"He's wearing the Chain of Infinite Protection," Ulbert whispered back.

"I think we should eat him anyway," Gilbert said sourly.

It was all very distressing, but despite his nervousness Albert had an inspiration. "Tomorrow the Queen will lay forty-eight thousand eggs!" he announced loudly.

Since the Queen laid forty-eight thousand eggs every day, it wasn't much of a prediction, but the assembled termites cheered loudly and this broke the tension. Albert sank comfortably into trance, had a vision of some new corridors in D-wing and everyone was happy.

After that it got easier. Albert would put on his robes, close his eyes and say exactly what he saw. The termites would cheer, the King would propose a vote of thanks, then everybody would go about their business.

But on the day of Fairy Nuff's garden party, it all went horribly wrong.

Eleven

Before it actually happened, Albert had no idea he was about to predict disaster. In fact he felt quite chipper.

"Nice day for a chew!" he greeted Bilbert, the termite whose job it was to help him with his robes.

"Chew-chew, chew-chew," Bilbert replied.

"Everybody gathered?" Albert asked.

"All present and correct," Bilbert confirmed. "King's on his throne, Queen sends her apologies: too busy laying eggs – what else is new? Your public's gathered, High Imperial Grand Termite Prophet. Got a good one for us today?"

"Expect so," Albert said. He never

knew what he would see until he saw it, but up to now his predictions had always been quite gratifying – new wood discovered, new galleries completed, fresh food sources, all that sort of thing.

Bilbert fussily arranged the folds of the robes and stepped back to check them. "That'll have to do," he said. "Don't want to keep people waiting. Good chewing!"

"Good chewing," Albert replied and walked out onto his prophet's dais. There was a short burst of applause before everyone fell silent.

Albert nodded to King Ethelbert, who nodded back.

"Let the prophecy commence!" proclaimed the King.

Albert shut his eyes, sank into trance and instantly saw something so terrifying that he felt his limbs stiffen and his blood run cold. He blinked without opening his eyes (a trick he'd picked up as a child) then re-ran the vision.

It was no less terrifying second time around.

Usually when Albert saw his visions he came out of trance at once and announced the good news right away. This time he spent so long, checking and re-checking that the King reached out and poked him with a twig.

"Get on with it!" King Ethelbert whispered.

Albert swam up out of trance and looked around in something close to panic.

"Your prediction," the King reminded him snappily. "Tell us your prediction."

"Agh," Albert began, making a strangled sound inside his throat. "Urr. Gaargh."

The King frowned. "Agh urr gaargh?" he asked. "What's that supposed to mean? Cough, man, cough – nobody can understand you!"

Albert coughed, knowing it would make no difference. "I ah— I ah— I ah—" he stammered. He began to rotate his head in the hope it might free his voice. He felt a twitch develop under his right eye. He wondered what would happen if he just ran away and hid.

King Ethelbert was losing patience. "Oh, just get on with it!"

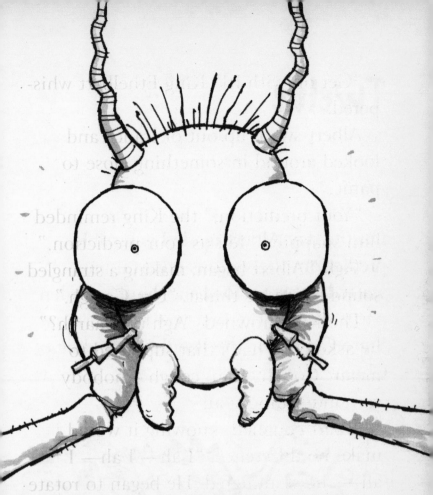

"Awa— awa— awa—" groaned Albert.
Then suddenly his panic popped and he
found he could speak again.

"The castle will explode today," he
cried. He looked around in horror.
"We're all going to die!"

Twelve

On the day Albert made his terrible prediction, the various entertainments started to arrive for Fairy Nuff's garden party. Among the first was the National State Circus for the People's Republic of China.

It was an unusually large circus since China is an unusually large country. Caravan after caravan moved at a stately pace through Bluebell Wood. Some contained acrobats. Some contained jugglers. Some contained pretty girls in boots and tights.

In front of them all, dictating the stately pace at which the line of caravans processed, walked the People's elephants. Each one was dressed up as a Chinese dragon since they played dragons in their act.

But while the costumes were colourful and entertaining, nobody would have mistaken the elephants for anything other than what they were. They walked like elephants. They had trunks like elephants. They had tails like elephants. They smelled like elephants.

It was the smell that caused all the excitement around the most dangerous thing in Bluebell Wood (except for Fairy Nuff's exploding castle) – a colony of ants that had fled from Africa to escape religious persecution.

While they lived on the Serengeti Plain, these ants ate only elephants. Since they came to Bluebell Wood, they'd had to manage on snowdrops, bluebells, daisies, honeysuckle and various root vegetables, depending on the season. But they longed for elephant meat and were hungry all the time.

Ant No. 287655439 was out jogging when the National State Circus for the People's Republic of China entered Bluebell Wood. A hauntingly familiar scent wafted past her on the breeze.

Ant No. 287655439 stopped dead and sniffed the air. For a moment she could scarcely believe her nose. Then the smell came again, along with the distant sound of elephant footfalls.

Cautiously, Ant No. 287655439 edged forward. The sound grew louder and the smell grew stronger. She could see very little since the grass was high in summer, but she climbed up a mulberry bush to give herself a better vantage point.

As she reached the top, the first of the great beasts appeared around a corner of the path.

The elephant was tarted up to look Chinese, but Ant No. 287655439 wasn't fooled for a minute. Her stomach turned a somersault and her mouth began to water. It was all she could do to stop from hurling herself on the elephant, mandibles snapping at the lovely meat. But she got a grip on herself and climbed down the mulberry bush instead. Then she hurried back to her anthill.

"You're home early," remarked Ant No. 833456321, who happened to be on sentry duty.

"Elephants!" gasped Ant No. 287655439 a little breathlessly. "I've just seen elephants!"

"No elephants in England," said Ant No. 833456321 severely. "The Queen Aunt Ant said so."

"Sniff the air! Sniff the air!" shouted Ant No. 287655439.

Ant No. 833456321 sniffed cautiously, then blinked. "Good grief, you're right!" she said.

Together they raced into the depths of the anthill to tell the Queen Ant, who ordered elephant hunters to be sent out at once.

Thirteen

While his castle was under construction, Fairy Nuff took a suite in the Ritz-Posh Hotel and vowed he wouldn't move into his new home until after the grand opening at the garden party.

So he ordered a chauffeur-driven limo to take him to Bluebell Wood at 10.30 on the morning of his garden party because he wanted to make sure everything was ready for his guests, who would be arriving at 11am.

The first thing he saw as he approached the wood was the life-size ice sculpture of King Kong and the Empire State Building towering above the treetops. It was taller than his castle and the sight somehow made him feel it was going to be a brilliant day.

The feeling was entirely wrong.

Fairy Nuff's troubles started when his PR person met him in the castle courtyard. She was wearing a BBC West of England Light Orchestra Fan Club T-shirt and carrying a clipboard.

"Have you heard the weather forecast?" she asked at once.

Fairy Nuff blinked. "No – is it going to rain?" He wasn't worried about rain

since he'd bought the Millennium Dome.

The PR person looked at him sadly. "Continuous sunshine all day. Temperatures of a hundred and five. It will be the hottest day in England since 1834."

"But that's good isn't it?" Fairy Nuff asked her. "People like a bit of sun."

"People used to like a bit of sun," the PR person corrected him. "But that was

before the hole in the ozone layer. A day like today will cook their brains. It doesn't matter about the ordinary guests of course, but we have the President of the United States coming. Imagine the state of the world if anything more happens to his brains."

"We'll give him a parasol," said Fairy Nuff decisively. "We'll give everybody parasols."

"Parasols ..." the PR person muttered as she wrote it down on her clipboard. She looked up again at Fairy Nuff. "What about King Kong?"

"He'd look silly with a parasol," said Fairy Nuff.

"He'll melt. The whole Empire State Building will melt, according to our calculations, somewhere around 3.30 in the afternoon."

"Doesn't matter," Fairy Nuff told her. "Everybody will be tired of it by then."

The PR person shook her head. "I'm afraid it does matter. The meltwater will flood the croquet lawn and cause the Titanic to sink again."

Fairy Nuff thought for a minute. "Arrange for teams of men to spray it with frozen carbon dioxide. That will stop it melting and make it all look nice and smoky."

"Frozen carbon dioxide ..." the PR

person muttered, writing it down. Fairy Nuff tried to sneak away, but she looked up and caught him. "The Fire Department are worried about our papier mâché Alps. They might catch alight in the heat and burn down Bluebell Wood."

"Arrange for teams of men to have them sprayed with water," Fairy Nuff said promptly.

"The Fire Department is also concerned about the papier mâché Statue of Liberty, Eiffel Tower, Parthenon, Coliseum, Pyramids, and Belgian chocolate factory."

"Have them sprayed as well." He eyed her cautiously. "Is that all?"

The PR person snapped the top onto her pen. "Mr Hong wants to see you."

Mr Hong was Most Equal Comrade-in-Charge of the National State Circus for the People's Republic of China. He bowed politely to Fairy Nuff.

"All our elephants have disappeared," he said.

Fourteen

"Have you looked under things?" asked Fairy Nuff.

"We have looked everywhere," said Mr Hong. "Deeply regret the National State Circus for the People's Republic of China will be unable to perform for your honoured guests today."

"What about the acts that don't need elephants?" asked Fairy Nuff.

"The acts that don't need elephants must help us look for the elephants," Mr Hong bowed again. "Deeply regret."

"That's all right," said Fairy Nuff. "It would have been nice to have a circus, but there's probably enough entertainment without it." He wondered where the elephants might have disappeared to. Then he wondered why Mr Hong was still standing there looking at him.

"We wish to be paid," said Mr Hong. "Deeply regret."

"But you're not performing," Fairy Nuff protested. "You've just told me."

"We've still come all the way from China," Mr Hong said reasonably. "Deeply regret expenses have accrued."

"Yes, I suppose so," Fairy Nuff said thoughtfully. He wasn't greatly worried – it was only money.

"Deeply regret we wish to be paid now," said Mr Hong.

Fairy Nuff's PR person appeared at his elbow. "About King Kong—" she whispered.

"Not now!" hissed Fairy Nuff. "I can't think about King Kong while I'm talking to Mr Hong. I'll deal with King Kong when Mr Hong has gone."

"It's Mr Long," the PR person insisted. "The sculptor of King Kong. I really do think you should talk to him before Mr Hong has gone."

"What have Mr Long and King Kong got to do with Mr Hong?" asked Fairy Nuff, bewildered.

"Mr Long has just been asked to do another sculpture. He has to fly out to Hong Kong at lunchtime and he wants to be paid for King Kong before he leaves. I thought it might be easier if you paid him and Mr Hong together."

Fairy Nuff stared at her for a moment. "You think I should pay Mr Long for King Kong before he flies out for Hong Kong and Mr Hong is long gone?"

"Yes."

"No problem," Fairy Nuff said.

"Mr Grogan of Grogan Papier Mâché would like some money too," his PR person told him. "He says they've got to pay their suppliers soon."

"No problem," Fairy Nuff said.

"The gardener called Ken who did your Zen has presented a bill for seven thousand point ten."

"No problem," Fairy Nuff said.

"The BBC want lunch money for their West of England Light Orchestra."

"No problem."

"Mr Branson has asked—"

"No problem," said Fairy Nuff.

"There's a deposit due for the Red Arrows."

"No problem."

"NASA needs a million dollars for fuel, Associated Associates are demanding their fee, the people who raised the Titanic claim their money is due, Disneyland Paris have sent their accountants—"

"No prob— Who are Associated Associates?" asked Fairy Nuff.

"Your PR people," his PR person told him.

"There's no problem with any of this," said Fairy Nuff. "If you hand me that wheelbarrow, I'll go and get their money now."

But when he reached the hollow tree with the two red Xs on it, all his cash and share certificates were gone.

Fifteen

Widow Buhiss also set out early for the garden party because she wanted time to hide the Crown Jewels before she revenged herself on Fairy Nuff.

Before she was jailed in the Tower of London, she lived on a rambling, poisonous, vermin-ridden estate beside Bluebell Wood. Orc thought she'd hide the jewels there, but the car they'd stolen hurtled past the gate.

Widow Buhiss aimed the Bentley convertible along the rutted road that led to Bluebell Wood.

"Is – this – where – you're – hiding – the – Crown – Jules?" Orc asked, bouncing like a Bishop in the back seat.

"Grrr – grrr – grrr – grrr," remarked Gestapo, bouncing beside him. Long journeys made him car-sick.

A dear sweet little bunny-rabbit hopped out onto the road. Widow Buhiss crashed the gears and jerked the steering wheel in an attempt to run it over. "Yes," she shouted over the shriek of the engine.

The rabbit leaped back just in time.

"Grrr," growled Gestapo in disappointment.

She found a narrow lane and floored the pedal. The Bentley bucked and skidded, one wheel in a ditch. They hit a bump and Gestapo threw up on Orc's lap. The car lost traction, spun round twice and struck a tree.

They climbed from the wreckage. "Don't make Bentleys like they used to," Widow Buhiss muttered. "Get the sack and follow me."

Orc retrieved the sack with the Crown Jewels from the car boot and trudged after her, Gestapo bouncing gaily at his heels. Behind them petrol fumes ignited and the car exploded.

"Excellent!" said Widow Buhiss. "They'll never track us now."

With Widow Buhiss in the lead, they tramped into the depths of Bluebell Wood. Eventually they came to a river. On the left was a wooden bridge that went from the near bank to the far bank. On the right was a metal bridge that went from the far bank to the near bank.

"Now we're getting somewhere!" she exclaimed, leaping onto the wooden bridge.

"Where we going?" Orc asked suspiciously. There was a colony of ants in Bluebell Wood that worried him.

"You'll see," Widow Buhiss told him gaily.

Moments later they reached a clearing with an anthill. Beside it was a hollow tree with two large red Xs on the trunk.

"The very place!" cried Widow Buhiss. "Only an idiot would come here with all those ants. We'll hide the jewels in that tree – the one somebody has marked for us. Bring the sack over here."

But Orc didn't move. He stayed frozen on the edge of the clearing. "I hate ants," he said.

"Oh, don't be such a Silly Billy!" Widow Buhiss exclaimed. She kicked the anthill with a pointed shoe. "See?" she said. "The ants are all asleep!"

"Don't care," Orc said. "I'm not moving."

"Oh, all right – I suppose I have to do everything myself as usual!" She flounced back and grabbed the sack.

When she dragged it over to the hollow tree, she found everything that Fairy Nuff had hidden there.

Sixteen

"Money!" shrieked Widow Buhiss. She started to stuff ten pound notes into her knickers but soon ran out of space. "Come here and help me carry this!" she ordered Orc.

"I'm not going near that anthill," Orc told her firmly.

Impatiently, Widow Buhiss tipped the Crown Jewels behind a nearby mulberry bush and started to push money into the empty sack.

"There's millions here!" she cried delightedly. "I'm rich! I'm rich! And you, as my employee, may consider yourself moderately well off."

The sight of all the cash gave Orc

some extra courage and he began to inch a little closer, his good eye firmly on the anthill.

"This changes everything," the Widow told him. "We can hide out in the Ritz-Posh Hotel – nobody would think of looking for us there. We can bribe people to lie about our where-abouts. We can hire a private army to overthrow the Government."

Gestapo gave a little growl as an ant

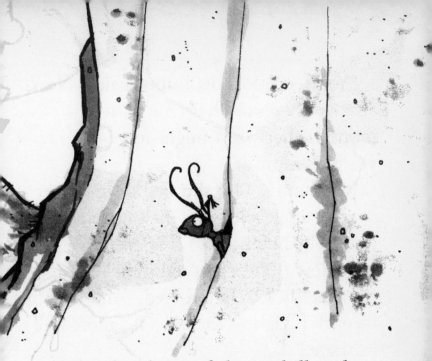

stuck her head out of the anthill and looked around, antennae quivering.

Orc jumped back as if he'd just been scalded. "I thought you said the ants were all asleep!"

"That little thing won't hurt you," Widow Buhiss told him scornfully. "It's more afraid of you than you are of it."

Orc doubted that, but after a moment the ant turned tail and disappeared back into the anthill.

"You see?" Widow Buhiss said. "Now get over here and help me with this money otherwise I might forget to pay you this month."

Reluctantly, Orc shuffled over. "Ants ate my uncle's leg off," he muttered under his breath.

Widow Buhiss ignored him. "Get it into the sack," she ordered. "And be sure to pack it tight – there's a lot more still in there."

Gestapo chased squirrels while Widow Buhiss watched Orc stuff money into the sack. After a while he said, "This isn't money."

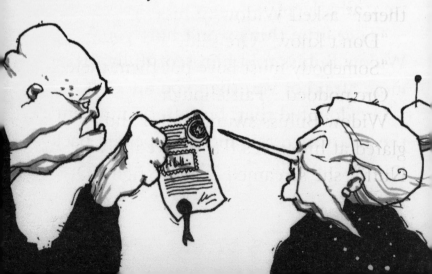

"Of course it is! It's millions of the finest British legal tender – I handled it myself."

"No," said Orc patiently. "The first lot was. But this stuff at the bottom isn't." He handed her a piece of paper. "See."

Widow Buhiss took the paper and stared at it closely. It was one of the gold mine shares her aunt had left her. "This is my money!" she breathed. "This is all my own money! Is there any more?"

Orc stuck his head back into the hollow tree. "Yus," he said.

"How do you imagine they got there?" asked Widow Buhiss

"Don't know," Orc said.

"Somebody must have put them there."

Orc nodded. "Fair enough."

Widow Buhiss swung round and glared at him, eyes flashing red. "Fairy Nuff?" she screamed. "You're right. Of course it's Fairy Nuff! It's always Fairy Nuff!!" She licked her lips. "You know what this means, don't you?"

"No," Orc told her warily.

She took such a deep breath that her eyes crossed and her chest swelled like a pigeon. There was a moments deep and profound silence.

Then ....

Then ....

Then ....

Then Widow Buhiss turned her face towards the heavens and released a mighty roar:

"I'm going to murder Fairy Nuff!"

Seventeen

Everybody panicked after Albert the termite issued his prediction.

"We're all going to be killed!" the cry went up. Termites began to run around aimlessly, chewing the air, chewing the floor, jumping high to try to chew the ceiling. One even chewed the left leg of the throne on which King Ethelbert was seated.

"Enough!" shouted King Ethelbert, listing to one side.

His subjects ignored him. One began a miserable Gaelic lament he'd learned from some Scottish sailor termites: "Ochone ... ochone ..." In moments the whole colony had taken it up. "Ochone ... ochone ... ochone ..."

But Ethelbert wasn't King for nothing. He stood up before his throne toppled over completely and took a breath so deep it swelled his thorax.

"Quiet!" he roared.

The wailing stopped at once and the termites in the Throne Room turned towards him in surprise.

"That's better," Ethelbert said. "Now just settle down and we'll consider this whole thing rationally." He turned to Albert. "First of all, are you quite sure what you saw?"

Albert nodded mournfully. "I'm afraid so, Your Majesty. It was the middle of the afternoon. The castle definitely exploded. Boom. Fire. Lumps flying all over the place. Burning wood. It was the end of the world – our bit of it anyway."

A nervous murmur ran through the gathered termites. King Ethelbert silenced it with a gesture. "Did you actually see termites killed?" he asked Albert.

"Oh yes, sir," Albert told him. "I saw collapsing corridors and great balls of fire rolling down our galleries and fleeing termites thrown into the air by the force of the explosion. The end of termite civilization as we know it. It was just like watching a disaster movie."

The nervous murmur returned, a notch or two higher in volume. King Ethelbert silenced it again. "Now this is important," he said to Albert. "Is there any way of avoiding this disaster?"

Albert blinked. He'd never considered the question before. All the predictions he'd made until now had been good, so nobody thought of avoiding them. Eventually he said, "I don't know, Your Majesty."

"What do you mean, you don't know?" snapped King Ethelbert irritably. "You're the High Imperial Grand Termite Prophet, aren't you?"

"Yes," said Albert miserably, "but I still don't know."

"Then you'd better find out," the King said ominously. "You'd better just get on your bike and find a way to save my empire. You think we came all the way from Java and settled here just to be blown up because of one of your stupid prophecies? You—"

"It wasn't because of one of my stupid prophecies," Albert said, appalled. "I don't do anything. I just see what's going to happen."

But the King wasn't listening. "As your King, I command you to leave at once – at once, mind – and find out how to stop the castle blowing up this afternoon. And when you've found out that, you're to stop it happening."

"But that means going into the Hideous Outside!" Albert protested.

"So it does," the King said nastily. "So it does."

Eighteen

The Hideous Outside was far worse than Albert had ever imagined. He chewed a hole in the ceiling of one of the upper galleries and squeezed through, stomach churning, into a truly ghastly world.

Ancient termite legends had different names for the Hideous Outside. One was 'the Land Forgotten by the Great Termite in the Sky'. Others were 'Horrorville' and 'Danger City, Arizona'. None did justice to the reality Albert now experienced.

First, there was a terrifying explosion of light. In contrast with the cosy darkness of the Beautiful Inside, the

Hideous Outside was filled with light, harsh, garish and penetrating. It struck him blind immediately so that he stood trembling and vulnerable, imagining the horrid sunshine must be stripping the flesh from his bones.

Fortunately the blindness only lasted a short time, but as his sight returned, a new horror dawned. He was surrounded by space. An open world stretched and stretched in every direction. There were no nice enclosing walls, no comfortable

ceilings within easy reach. The only wood
to chew was directly underneath his feet.

For an instant Albert panicked. He
spun around and tried to dive back into
the hole he'd chewed through the
gallery ceiling. But already it was closed
over, sealed by the quick-drying wood
glue applied by Gilbert, Ulbert, Dilbert,
Bilbert and Cuthbert, the five termites
deputised to escort him to the bound-
aries of his mission. Albert gave a little
wail of terror.

He was standing on a vast plain of wood that he recognised as the floorboards of the castle. For a moment he considered chewing his way back into the Beautiful Inside, but the Chain of Infinite Protection had been stripped from his neck and without it he'd certainly be eaten if he returned without an answer to his terrifying vision.

Albert shivered violently. He wished he'd never met the termite in the turban.

But he knew regrets would get him nowhere, so he pulled himself together and began to search for the reason the castle was going to explode.

First he examined the nearest wall. The mortar between the stones smelt peculiar, but apart from that he could find nothing amiss.

Then he began a determined hunt for a very large bomb, but found no sign of that either.

After that, he examined room after room, inspecting the panelling, the furnishings, the ornaments, the freshly painted walls, the newly carpeted floors, the pictures, doors, windows – everything, in fact, there was to see.

There were a lot of rooms and he was exhausted by the time he finished, but still no nearer finding what he needed to know.

At last it became clear the answer was not in the castle itself and Albert steeled himself. Although the inside of the castle was the Hideous Outside for someone brought up in the Beautiful Inside, he knew there was an Even More Hideous Outside beyond the confines of the castle.

And if the answer wasn't in the Hideous Outside inside the inside of the castle, then it had to be in the Even More Hideous Outside outside the inside of the castle.

Albert straightened his spine. He could put it off no longer. He had his orders from the King. He had his duty to his fellow termites. There was only one way he could fulfil his destiny.

He scuttled from the Hideous Outside to the Even More Hideous Outside outside the Hideous Outside.

And there, oddly enough, he met the true love of his life.

Nineteen

Fairy Nuff made his way slowly back through Bluebell Wood wondering what he was going to do.

He owed Murphy O'Toole two hundred million pounds for building his nice new castle. He owed various companies another five million or so for antiques to furnish it. The painters had put in a bill for two hundred and fifty thousand pounds. Double glazing was another million and a half.

Carpeting accounted for three million more, central heating two million and three quarters, fuel for central heating a round half million.

The Van Gogh over the mantelpiece was thirty million, the dining table, specially made, was fifty thousand pounds. The burglar alarm system was a quarter of a million, electrical fittings were four million, insurance one million. Even doorknobs somehow amounted to three quarters of a million, possibly because Fairy had ordered them in solid gold.

Then there was the garden party.

The National State Circus for the People's Republic of China wanted to be paid in Chinese yuan, but even so the cost was just short of two million sterling. The ice sculpture of King Kong was a cool eight million. The various papier mâché bits and pieces came to more than fifteen million altogether.

The Titanic was a bargain at eight hundred thousand pounds for the one-day hire, but transport costs were extra and these amounted to four million. The BBC West of England Light Orchestra had forty-eight members who were claiming two hundred pounds each. The President of the United States had sub-mitted expenses of one million, seven hundred and seventy-six thousand, five hundred and forty-five dollars.

Catering, by Harrods, was three million (but the food was guaranteed organic), the final bill for the Red Arrows would be five hundred thou-sand, much the same as Mr Branson was charging for the hire of his jumbo.

NASA was the really big one. Building a launch pad and hiring the space shuttle cost, at five hundred and two million, seven hundred and fifty thousand dollars, even more than the castle itself. Disneyland Paris cost three million. Associated Associates, the PR people, wanted another million.

He'd run up quite a large account at the Ritz-Posh Hotel. He didn't know the up-to-date amount, but the last time he looked, it was running at four hundred and fifty-one thousand pounds.

Fairy Nuff fumbled in his pocket and found a five pence piece.

It was well after eleven by the time he reached the garden party so almost all the guests were there. He noted with horror they were demolishing vast quantities of food and drink.

His PR person spotted him at once and hurried over. She eyed the empty wheelbarrow with a look of deep suspicion. "Sir Fairy—" she began.

"Get me a microphone," Fairy told her. "I have to speak to my guests."

"But my fee—" she protested. "The

people who want to be paid—"

"A microphone," said Fairy firmly. "And something to stand on."

She gave him the same look of deep suspicion she had given the wheelbarrow, but went off all the same. Out of the corner of his eye, he could see his creditors queuing up. There seemed to be even more of them than there were guests.

The PR person returned with a microphone and an old orange crate. She handed him the microphone and turned the orange crate upside down for him to stand on. Fairy Nuff took a deep breath and climbed up.

"Ladies and gentlemen," he said into the microphone. He paused while his voice echoed through the loudspeaker system. It was state of the art, hired for the occasion at a cost of eighty-two thousand pounds.

"Ladies and gentlemen," Fairy Nuff said again. "Mr Prime Minister, Mr President, Mr Poet Laureate, honoured guests, I would like to welcome you to my garden party." He paused while everybody cheered. When the noise died down, he licked his lips and said, "I may not have mentioned it, but there's a cover charge of—" He made a quick calculation, swallowed, then went on, "— two and a half million pounds per head for all those of you who want to enjoy the entertainments, food and facilities, including standing on my grass."

There was a thunderous silence. Several hundred eyes glared at him threateningly.

Fairy Nuff swallowed again. "Well,

not exactly a cover charge," he said. "More a voluntary donation."

The silence remained thunderous.

"Just feel free to give what you can – a million, a few hundred thousand, anything would help – to, ah, well to my PR person or any member of Associated Associates, or even Mr Hong of the Peoples ..." He trailed off. The only sound in his vast garden was the last fading echo of his own voice on the loudspeaker system.

Fairy Nuff jumped off the orange crate and fled.

Twenty

When Widow Buhiss kicked the anthill with her pointed shoe, the ants inside were not asleep.

Actually they were having a party.

Since it was a party to celebrate the capture of a herd of elephants – all netted and tethered despite their cunning camouflage as Chinese dragons – it was a pretty wild affair.

The Queen Ant ordered free beer for the workers. The Queen Mother Ant donated eighteen cases of her favourite port, mainly because she wanted to make sure there was something she could drink herself.

The Queen Aunt Ant, an altogether more generous sort, produced a barrel of twenty-year-old single malt Highland whiskey, thirty flagons of gin, a small bottle of Curaçao, three hundred cases of vintage Bollinger, a crate of brandy and an old-fashioned book on how to mix cocktails.

It was the champagne cocktails that did for Ant No. 287655439. The bubbles went straight to her antennae and she became extremely silly.

She pinned KISS ME QUICK notices to the backs of soldier ants and tried to trip them up as they marched past.

She stood by the door of the ladies'

loo and engaged her friends in lengthy conversations when they were desperate to go in.

She played Adam-and-Eve-and-Pinch-Me with everybody fool enough to fall for it.

She crept up behind important ants and tickled them.

She gripped ants by the arm and insisted on telling them a truly dreadful joke about three frogs who spent the night in a house, even though most of them had heard it before and weren't amused the first time.

She tried to entertain large groups of ants by doing a funny walk which involved her standing up on her back legs, knees bent, and striding forward shouting "I'm a gee-raff! I'm a gee-raff!"

When she got tired of that – and rather sore from falling over – she began to sing. She started with a rousing chorus of 'The Lion Sleeps Tonight' to remind everyone of their African origins and was in the middle of 'Widdicomb Fair' when Widow Buhiss kicked the anthill.

"... with Peter Gurney, Peter Davey, Dan'l Whitten, Harry Hawk—" Ant No. 287655439 sang tunelessly.

"What was that?" the Queen Ant asked suspiciously.

"— Old Uncle Tom Cobleeeeey and aaaall!" wailed Ant No. 287655439.

"Why don't you have Ant No.

287655439 go and find out," advised her Chief Adviser quickly.

"Excellent idea," the Queen Ant nodded. "Go and find out who's kicking our hill, Ant No. 287655439," she ordered. Then, as an afterthought, she added, "Quietly."

"Yes, Majesty!" Ant No. 287655439 saluted briskly and scurried off.

Since she was prone to losing her way even when she wasn't awash with champagne cocktail, it took her quite a time to find the anthill entrance and when she looked out, her eyes wouldn't focus properly.

It was like watching fish underwater. There was an ugly dog thing growling fiercely. There was an ugly human male type person who jumped back in horror when he saw her. There was an ugly female human person filling up a sack with bits of paper.

"I thought you said the ants were all asleep!" the ugly human male type person shouted.

"That little thing won't hurt you," the ugly female human person told him. "It's more afraid of you than you are of it."

That wasn't true, of course. Ant No. 287655439 wasn't afraid of anything at the moment. In fact she felt she would never be afraid of anything ever again. But none of the three outside looked much of a threat to the colony, so she ducked back inside and scuttled off to tell the Queen Ant there was nothing to worry about.

Unfortunately she took a wrong turning somewhere and ended up back at the entrance. By this time, the two ugly humans and the ugly dog were gone.

In their place, standing on a leaf, was the most handsome insect Ant No. 287655439 had ever seen. He was pure white and wonderfully exotic.

She fell in love with him at once.

Twenty-One

"This way!" cried Widow Buhiss, dancing along the path in Bluebell Wood. Orc shuffled behind her, weighed down by the massive sack of money.

"Couldn't we hide this somewhere?" he asked grumpily. "Until after we murder Fairy Nuff?"

"If you think I'm going to let that money out of my sight again, you're even madder than you look," Widow Buhiss snapped. "Don't set it down for an instant."

"But how are we going to kill him if I haven't even got my hands free?"

"Something will turn up," Widow Buhiss said. "Something will present itself."

Up ahead, Gestapo started to bark furiously.

"What's wrong with that stupid dog?" asked Widow Buhiss impatiently. "Go and see what he wants."

"Will you mind the sack?" Orc asked.

"Of course I won't mind the sack!" Widow Buhiss told him. "I'm just a poor weak old widow woman while you're a hulking ugly great brute of a man without much brains."

Orc tramped stoically up to where Gestapo was barking, the sack weighing

more and more heavily with every step. "It's elephants," he called back.

Widow Buhiss blinked. "What?"

"Elephants," Orc repeated. "He's barking at elephants."

Widow Buhiss frowned. "There aren't any elephants in England."

"Are now," Orc said. "Chinese by the look of them."

"No such thing as Chinese elephants!" Widow Buhiss told him sharply. All the

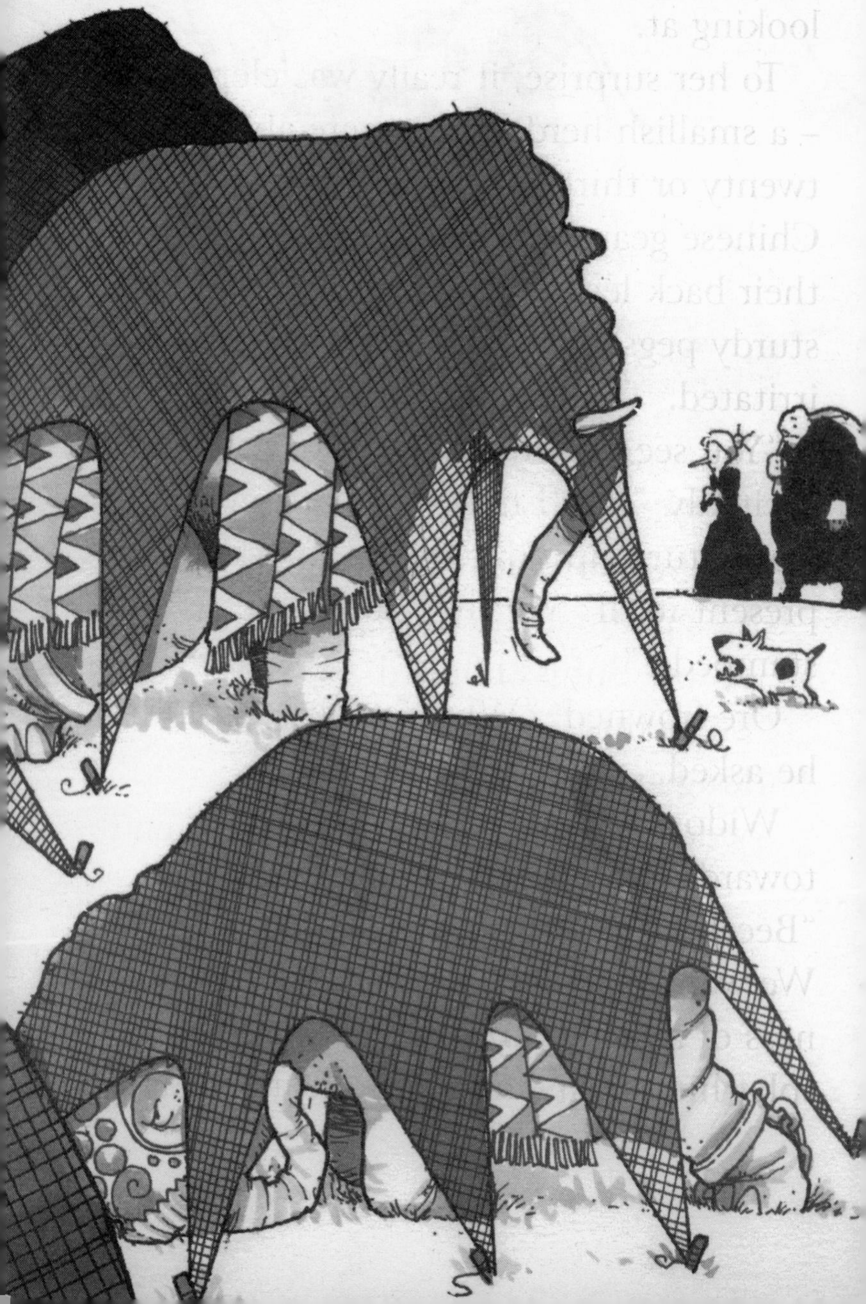

same, she came up to see what he was
looking at.

To her surprise, it really was elephants
– a smallish herd. There were about
twenty or thirty of them, dressed in
Chinese gear, captured under nets with
their back legs secured to the ground by
sturdy pegs. They all looked extremely
irritated.

"You see?" Widow Buhiss exclaimed
excitedly. "Did I not say that something
would turn up, that something would
present itself? We shall start an elephant
stampede!"

Orc frowned. "Why shall we do that?"
he asked.

Widow Buhiss turned her eyes
towards the treetops in impatience.
"Because we want to crush Fairy Nuff.
We want to pulverise him to the thickness of a crêpe Suzette. We want to
splat him, dismember him, distribute his

remains across seven counties. Stampeding elephants are very good at that."

"But how do you know they'll stampede over him?" Orc asked.

"Because I shall lead the stampede!"
Widow Buhiss cried. "I shall lead them
to his rotten garden party. I shall ride
the foremost elephant. I learned how
to be a mahout when my poor dear
departed husband was in the Indian
Army."

She ran across and cut the netting
from the largest elephant, then quickly
climbed onto his back. The elephant
glanced round at her and started ner-
vously at what he saw, but couldn't run
off since he was still tethered.

"See how skilfully I mount!" Widow
Buhiss called to Orc. "See how expertly
I control this mighty beast! See how
affectionate he is towards me!" She
poked the elephant behind the ear and

he tried vainly to hurl her off his back.

"A cry of M-I-C-E will stampede them utterly," Widow Buhiss said. "I learned in India that all elephants are terrified of M-I-C-E. You and Gestapo had better follow us as best you can."

She stood up on the back of her elephant and pointed dramatically in a forward direction. "Release the elephants!" she ordered.

Since she seemed distracted, Orc risked setting the money sack down before he went round the elephants removing their netting and untethering them from their stakes.

"They're released," he announced when he had finished.

"Stand clear!" Widow Buhiss called.

Orc moved behind a tree. "Standing clear," he confirmed.

"Gestapo, stand clear!" Widow Buhiss shouted.

Gestapo moved behind a different tree. "Woof," he said.

"Shout M-I-C-E," Widow Buhiss instructed.

"M-I-C-E!" shouted Orc obediently.

"Shout the word – don't spell it!" Widow Buhiss screamed.

"MICE!!" bellowed Orc.

The elephants stampeded.

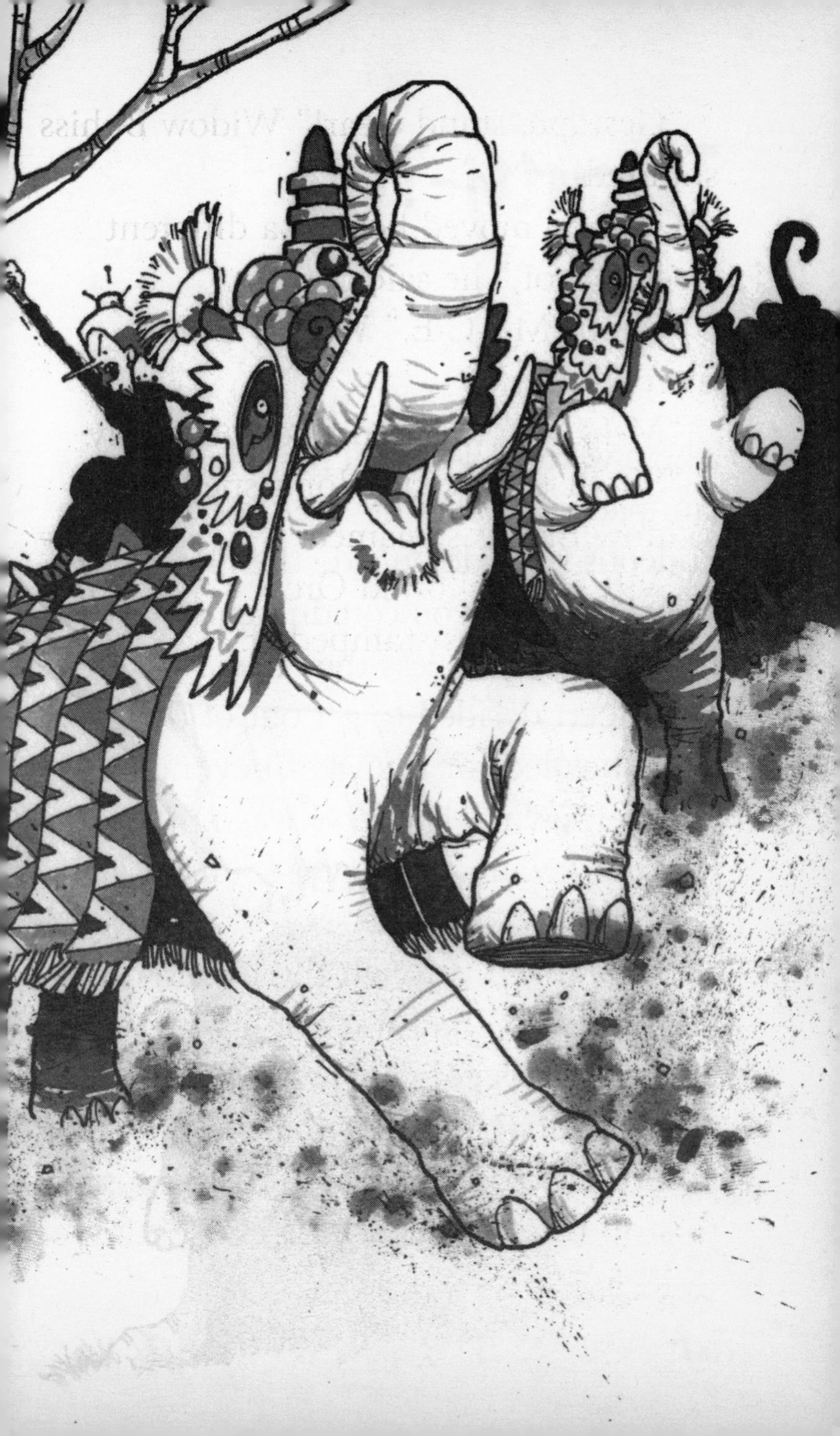

Twenty-Two

There were wall-to-wall human beings jam-packed in the the Even More Hideous Outside outside the Hideous Outside. Since you couldn't chew through human beings unless they had a wooden leg, Albert decided to get out of their way.

He headed for the trees beyond the croquet lawn. The wood was nothing like the Javanese rainforest, but at least it felt a bit like home.

As he hiked through the undergrowth, he realized he had not the least idea where he was going or what he was going to do. He knew what he was supposed to do all right. He was supposed to stop the end of termite civilization as he knew it. But how that might be done, he had not the least idea.

He came to a clearing and climbed onto a leaf to have a little think.

There was an odd sort of structure in front of him. It was nearly eight feet high and very well designed since there were no windows to let in the Hideous Outside. The material it was made from looked even stronger than wood. He wondered if a British termite millionaire had built it.

He was still wondering when out of the building popped the most beautiful insect he had ever seen. She was wonderfully exotic with long, slim antennae, liquid eyes and large, pert mandibles.

He fell in love with her at once.

Albert did what termites always do when they discover they're in love. He did a little dance, wiggling his bottom in the direction of his beloved.

To his joy she responded, scuttling down the outside of her home to get a closer look at him. She even did a little dance of her own when she was within striking distance of his leaf.

"I love you!" called down Albert, who didn't believe in beating about the bush when it came to affairs of the heart.

"I love you too!" she called back, then blushed, hiccoughed and fell over.

Albert jumped from his leaf, rushed across and helped her up. "Are you all right, my darling?" he asked solicitously.

The beautiful creature giggled. "Never better," she told him and snuggled up into his arms.

"What's your name?" asked Albert.

"Ant No. 287655439," said Ant No. 287655439. "What's yours?"

"Albert," Albert told her. "High Imperial Grand Termite Prophet and loyal subject of King Ethelbert."

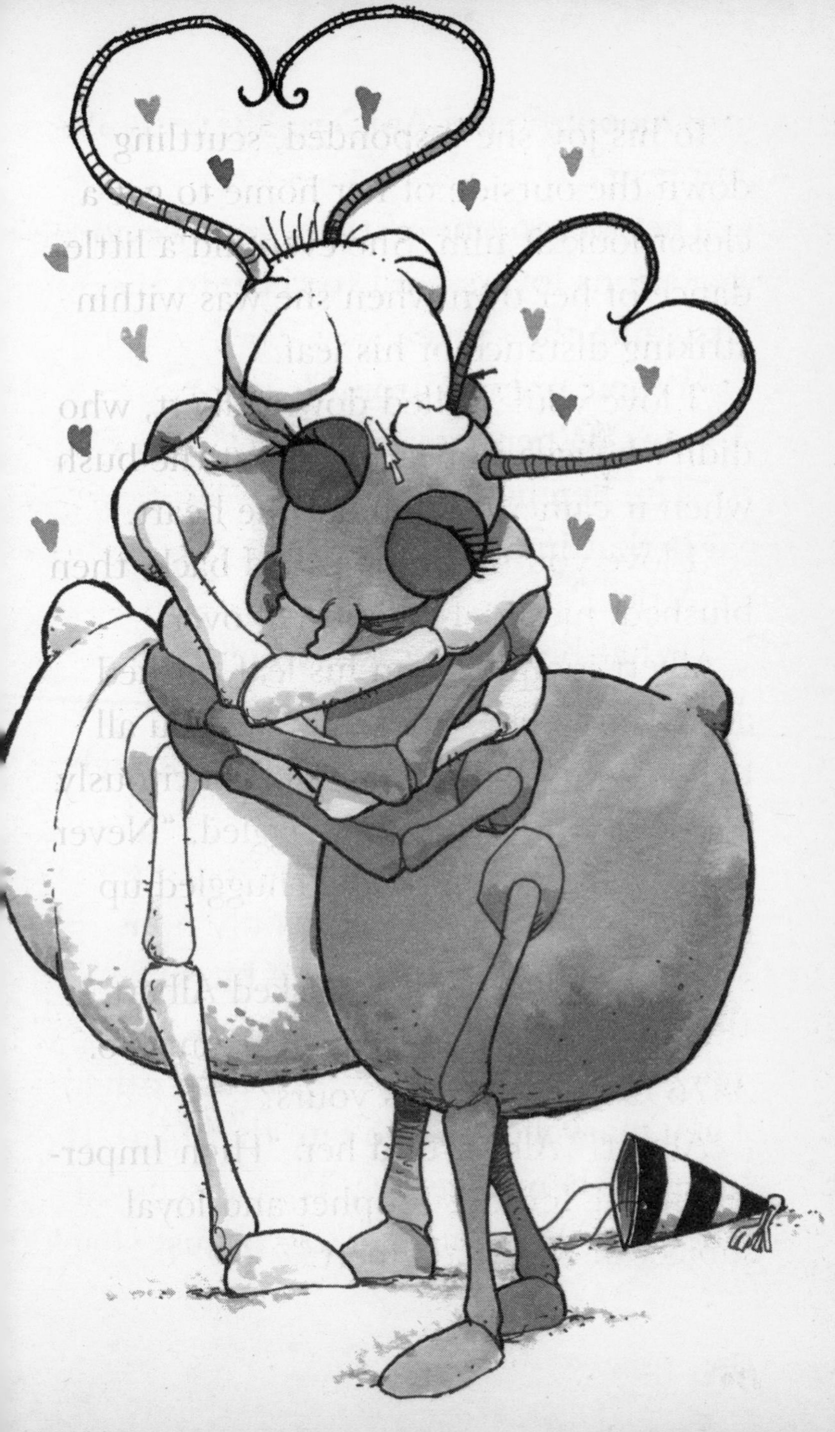

"Oooooh," said Ant No. 287655439, impressed.

They began one of those intense conversations lovers tend to get into the first time they meet.

"Where are you from?"

"Java. Where are you from?"

"The Serengeti Plain."

"Is that in Sheffield?"

"Africa."

"What brought you to Bluebell Wood?"

"Religious persecution. What brought you to Bluebell Wood?"

"Two lumberjacks."

And so on and so on, mainly nonsense which didn't matter a bit since they were happy in each other's arms. They spoke of their love for each other. They marvelled at the fate that had brought them together. They discussed whether they should marry or just shack up and decided marriage was much nicer. But suddenly Albert went quiet.

"What's the matter, sweetums?" asked Ant No. 287655439 at once.

"We can't get married," Albert told her dolefully.

Ant No. 287655439 pulled away from him. "Why not?" she demanded. A horrible suspicion dawned on her. "Is there another ant?"

"Nothing like that." Albert shook his head. "It's just that my people live in a castle that's going to explode quite soon. I have to find some way to save them and I don't think I can do it."

"Don't be silly," Ant No. 287655439 told him briskly. "Your people can move in with us. There's lots of room since we built our new extension."

She leaned forward and gave him a little kiss. "You stay here while I go and arrange things with the Queen Ant."

Twenty-Three

"After him!" cried Fairy Nuff's creditors as Fairy Nuff legged it across the croquet lawn.

"Stop, thief! Give us our money!" they roared, hurling things in his general direction.

Garden party guests put down their drinks to watch, wondering if Fairy Nuff would get away.

It was now mid afternoon – almost 3.30pm – and very, very hot. The sun beat down relentlessly and Fairy Nuff's new castle began quietly to smoke.

Fairy Nuff dived into the fog caused by the workmen spraying frozen carbon dioxide on the life-sized ice sculpture of

King Kong climbing the Empire State Building.

"He's getting away!" screamed Mr Hong.

"Stop spraying!" the PR person formerly known as Fairy Nuff's PR person ordered the workmen. "You're not going to get paid."

The workmen stopped at once and put away their gear. In a moment the fog dissipated and King Kong started to melt. Fairy Nuff raced to hide behind the towering bulk of the Titanic.

The garden party guests cheered him on – this was better than all the other entertainments put together. Led by Mr Hong and Fairy Nuff's former PR person, the creditors thundered after him.

The tiny curl of smoke emerging from the battlements of Fairy Nuff's new castle got a little larger.

There was a flurry of activity close to the castle gate. Softly at first, but growing louder, there could be heard a marching chant of chew-chew, chew-chew!

"What's the matter?" asked the American President as two of his Secret Service bodyguards grabbed him and bundled him towards a waiting limo.

"Termites, Mr President!" one told him urgently.

The President glanced over his shoulder to see an enormous termite swarm emerge from the castle led by an unsteady ant. "Good grief!" exclaimed the President. "And me with a wooden leg!"

Pedestrians leaped out of the way as his limo took off at high speed. They watched for a moment, then screamed as they too saw the termite swarm. Everyone began to run in all directions, led by those with wooden body parts.

Soon there was nothing left of the garden party except Fairy Nuff and his creditors whose determination to get their money back far outweighed their fear of being chewed by termites. But despite their fearsome chant, the termites ignored them and marched directly into Bluebell Wood.

As his creditors closed in on him, Fairy Nuff decided to follow the termites.

Behind him, the smoke plume on the castle battlements grew larger.

Fairy Nuff broke from cover and raced for the safety of the wood.

"There he goes!" cried Mr Hong. Seven long-distance acrobats from the

State Circus of the People's Republic of China took up the chase, tumbling and cartwheeling as they did so. The remaining creditors piled in behind them.

Fairy Nuff redoubled his efforts, but long before he reached the safety of the trees, the acrobats overtook him. They swept around him in a cunning flanking movement, then backflipped to a halt and formed a sturdy little wall of China.

Fairy Nuff stopped, his eyes on the line of acrobats. Behind him he could hear the other creditors closing in. There was a pounding in his ears as he wondered what on earth to do.

He looked to his left. He looked to his right. There was no escape.

Suddenly he realised the pounding wasn't in his ears at all. The whole ground shook beneath his feet as a herd of stampeding elephants burst out of Bluebell Wood.

"Yipes!" yelled the acrobats as they saw the elephants.

"Yipes!" yelled the creditors for much the same reason.

Creditors and acrobats took to their heels.

"There he is!" screamed Widow Buhiss astride the leading elephant. She pointed straight at Fairy Nuff. "Pulverise him to the thickness of a crêpe Suzette! Splat him! Dismember him! Distribute his remains across seven counties!"

The elephants and Widow Buhiss were too close now for Fairy Nuff to get away.

But the leading elephant had had enough of Buhiss on his back.

He stopped dead and arched horribly so that she shot over his head, still screaming orders, and landed with a dull thud on the croquet lawn.

Trumpeting loudly, the elephants swung round and disappeared back into Bluebell Wood, narrowly missing Orc and Gestapo who were just emerging.

Widow Buhiss did a forward roll and leaped to her feet in a karate crouch.

"Never mind," she howled, "I'll dismember him myself." So saying, she launched herself towards the hapless Fairy.

At this point, Fairy Nuff's exploding castle finally exploded.

Twenty-Four

There were no termites near the castle when the castle exploded.

They'd all marched off (chanting 'Chew-chew, chew-chew') to their new home with the ants.

Albert was made especially welcome because of his prophetic powers. Just minutes after he arrived, the Queen Aunt Ant asked him for a Tarot reading.

This proved so successful that she persuaded the Queen Ant to allow Albert to make joint predictions for both ants and termites when he made his public appearances as High Imperial Grand Termite Prophet.

The first time he did so, he predicted a long and happy relationship between the termites and the ants in Bluebell Wood, with the exception of the termite Gilbert who seemed destined to choke to death while trying to eat one of his fellow termites.

But that was quite a long time in the future.

There were no ants near the castle when the castle exploded.

Apart from Ant No. 287655439, who was leading the termites, they were all in their anthill cleaning up, turning down beds and generally preparing for their guests.

Among those preparations was a tastefully decorated honeymoon suite for Ant No. 287655439 and Albert. Even when Ant No. 287655439 sobered up, she found she was still in love with Albert and they were married at once in an elaborate ceremony involving a great deal of drumming and a dance by everybody into what Albert still called the Hideous Outside.

There were no elephants near the castle when the castle exploded.

Once they'd disabused themselves of Widow Buhiss, they stampeded right back through Bluebell Wood, out the other side, down the N87 and finally ended up in Southampton where they stowed away on a boat to Africa and were never seen again.

There were almost no people near the

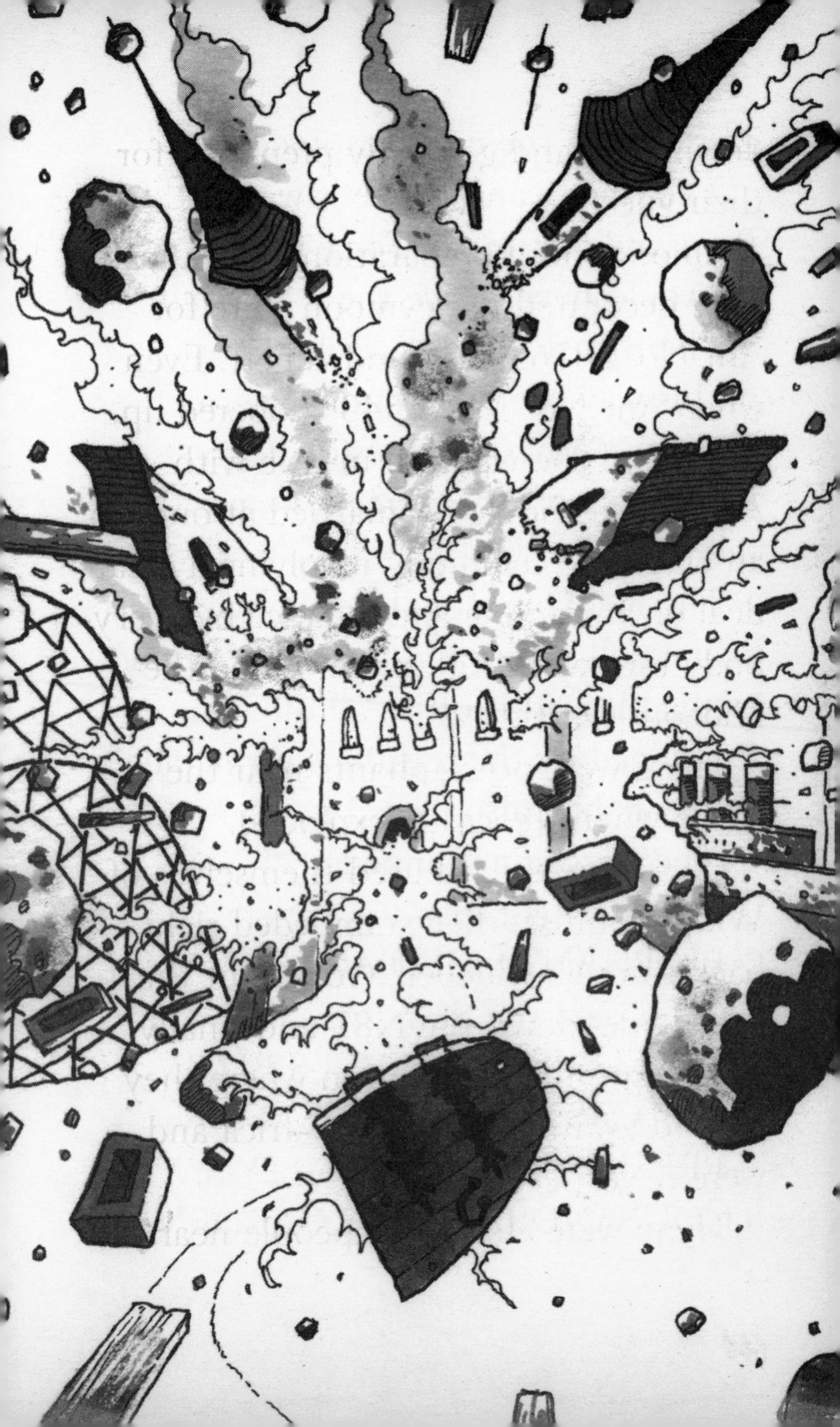

castle when the castle exploded.

The American President was at thirty thousand feet in Air Force One, vowing he would never leave the USA again.

The British Prime Minister was on his way back to London by car. Once the American President left, there was nobody he really wanted to talk to.

The media personalities, movie stars, peers, politicians and assorted freeloaders had legged it off in all directions, frightened by the termite swarm. The creditors had also legged it, frightened by the elephant stampede.

The story got into the papers.

ELEPHANT-SIZED ANTS TRAMPLE SEVEN said the Star.

TERRORIST TERMITES BLOW UP FAIRY CASTLE claimed the Mirror.

PRESIDENT PERSONALLY SAVES THOUSANDS AT BRIT GARDEN

PARTY reported the New York Herald Tribune.

In all the fuss and bother, there were only four living souls close to Fairy Nuff's exploding castle when Fairy Nuff's exploding castle finally exploded.

Three of them were Widow Buhiss, Orc, and pitbull terrier Gestapo.

The fourth (and nearest) was Fairy Nuff himself.

Twenty-Five

The force of the explosion swept Fairy Nuff off his feet and hurled him high into the air. He was carried over Widow Buhiss's head and flung beyond his castle grounds into the very heart of Bluebell Wood.

There was a moment of confusion as he tumbled, then a moment of panic as he fell. Twigs and branches scratched him as he plummeted towards the ground.

"Yeeaaaaaaaagh!" screamed Fairy Nuff, certain he was heading for a splatted death.

But it turned out he was wrong. As he closed his eyes and waited for the end,

something broke his fall. He opened his
eyes again to find he'd come down in
the middle of a mulberry bush on the
edge of the very clearing where he used
to hide his money in the hollow tree.

Fairy Nuff looked around. There was
a strange drumming sound coming from
the nearby anthill, but he had no time
to investigate. He had to find out if
Widow Buhiss was still after him or
whether she'd been blown up too.

He examined himself carefully to make sure nothing was broken then climbed out of the bush, picking mulberries from his hair. As he did so, there was the distant sound of something crashing through the undergrowth.

"Don't let him get away!" he heard Widow Buhiss call.

Fairy Nuff froze. If she found him now he was a goner for sure. He dived behind the bush and tried to make himself as small as possible. Something poked into his bottom, but he was too terrified to move.

The crashing sound drew closer. Orc and Widow Buhiss blundered into the clearing. Their clothes were tattered and their faces blackened and they looked more angry than Fairy Nuff had ever seen them.

"He fell somewhere around here – search the clearing," Widow Buhiss ordered Orc. "I'll go on ahead and steal another car."

"What happens if I can't find him?" Orc asked her, frowning.

"We'll just have to murder him some other time," Widow Buhiss snapped. "Don't take all day – we have to be out of here before the police come to investigate that stupid explosion." She raced off at top speed towards the road.

Orc began to search.

Fairy Nuff crouched down further despite the pain in his bottom. He held his breath and crossed his fingers, praying fervently that Orc would give up quickly and follow Widow Buhiss. But Orc didn't give up quickly. He searched thoroughly and poked in every bush.

Worse still he was getting closer.

"Come out, come out wherever you are," Orc sang quietly as he moved closer still. He broke a branch from a tree and started to beat the undergrowth with it.

The drumming in the anthill grew a little louder, but Orc, despite his fear of ants, was not distracted. He got so close that it was possible to see the hairs on his legs.

Orc stopped suddenly and sniffed. "What's this?" he said aloud. He turned and stared directly at the bush behind which Fairy Nuff was crouched. A horrible slow smile crossed his face. "That's where you are!" he said.

Clutching his tree branch like a club, Orc began to lumber straight towards the mulberry bush. "Got you now!" he called. "Got you now!"

He was almost on top of Fairy Nuff when a horde of ants swarmed from the anthill. They spread like a living carpet out across the clearing.

"Yeeeek!" shrieked Orc as he spotted

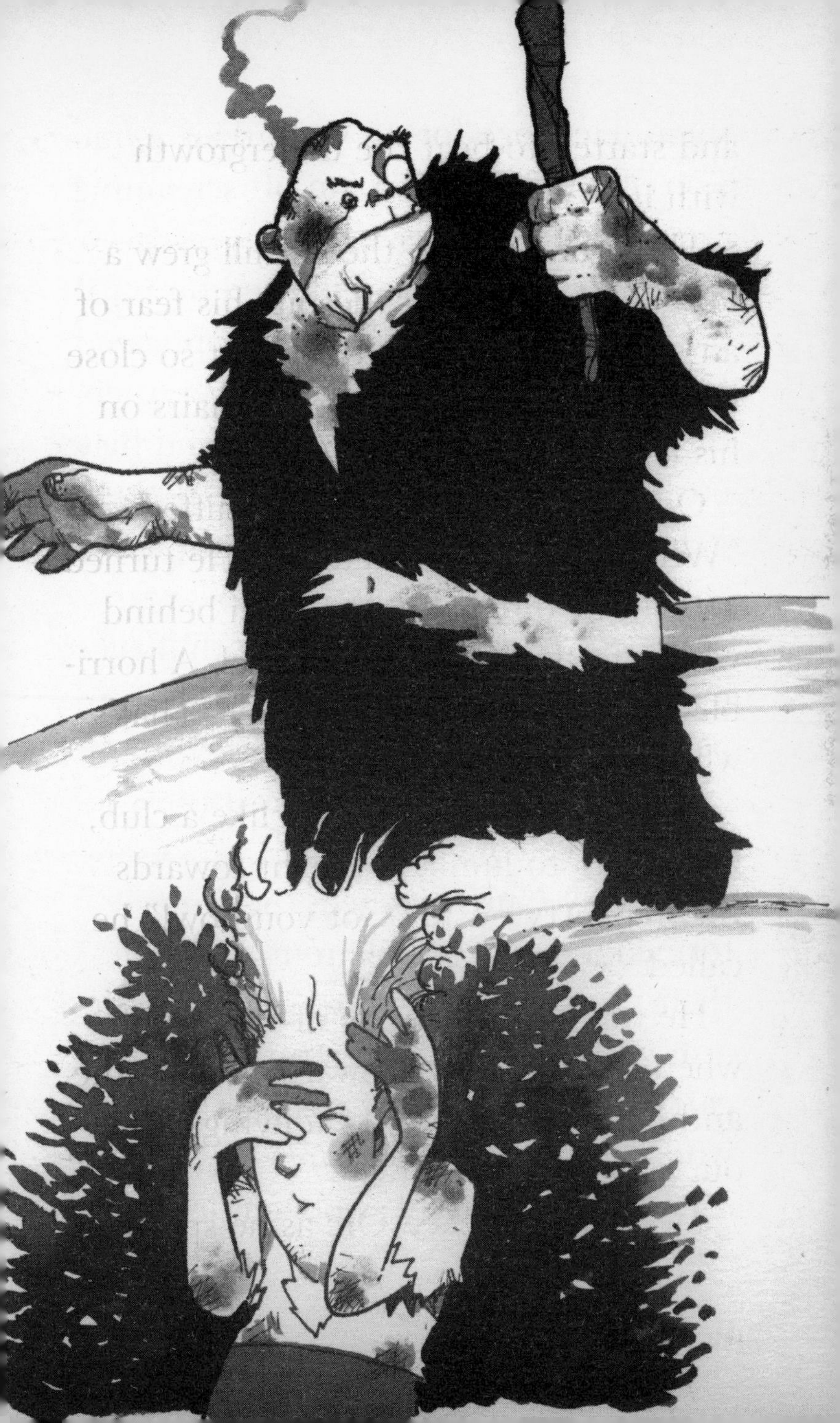

them. He froze for no more than a fraction of a second then ran off screaming after Widow Buhiss.

Fairy Nuff stayed scrunched up until the screams grew faint and disappeared. He waited a few moments longer, then cautiously peered out from behind his bush.

There were several hundred thousand ants half filling the clearing now with more still pouring from the anthill every minute, but somehow they didn't seem particularly threatening.

If anything they looked as if they might be celebrating.

As Fairy Nuff watched, the ants formed a moving circle round one of their number who was standing arm in arm with a large white termite. Ants carrying bongo drums emerged and the whole horde began to dance.

After a while they swooped down on

the two in the centre of the circle and carried them shoulder high back into the anthill.

Fairy Nuff waited until the last ant had disappeared before he dared stand up.

That's when he discovered the Crown Jewels had been poking up his bottom.

Epilogue

There was a special State Reception when Fairy Nuff delivered the Crown Jewels to Buckingham Palace.

"We're very glad to see those," the Queen told him as he handed them across. "Now we can get out again. We've already missed seven dinner parties and a hunt ball as it is."

"Sorry I took so long to get here, Your Majesty," Fairy Nuff apologised. "I had to come by bike."

The Queen sighed sympathetically. "Yes, we heard you've lost all your money and your castle has blown up. Perhaps this will help." She handed him

a parchment envelope embossed with
the royal crest.

Fairy Nuff looked at it and frowned.
It felt like there might be a cheque
inside. "What's this, Your Majesty?"

The Queen smiled broadly. "It's your reward for finding our Crown Jewels. It should pay off your creditors with just enough left over to build yourself another home." She tapped the side of her nose and winked at him. "Just make sure next time you use real cement – 'nuff said?"

"'Nuff said, Your Majesty," said Fairy Nuff.